Devour

By Rayne Havok

Rights

Summary

They came to my door and I knew right away that that was it. I knew that day was coming and still made no attempt to hide what had been done.

The police ask their questions and I don't answer. My answers wouldn't make them understand... maybe you will.

Warning

I'm told this book should have an 'extreme' warning.

Because these things are always in my head and on my mind, I don't always consider them to be over- the- top. To some it may be run- of- the mill and to others it may be too much.

If you feel like you may have issues reading 'extreme' stories please do not bother with this one, you may be offended.

I do not condone any of this shit in real life, please remember this is a work of fiction and as always do not try this at home.

Chapter One

Today...

"Mrs. Winthrop, I need you to initial at the bottom of this page, stating that you've heard and understand your rights as we've gone over them."

I can't for the life of me understand how I let myself end up here, how this cold dark room in the police station is where I've spent the night, interrogated by two asshole cops who look dumb enough to pee against the wind. I wish they would, it could give me a smile that would last a lifetime. Instead, their cocky, shit eating grins are going to be ingrained in my mind.

I feel so tired. I wish this whole night was over and that I was sleeping, whether it be in my own bed or some shitty mattress they set up for people here– I wouldn't care either way. I would sell my soul to the devil, right now, for a three-minute nap. But that's how they do things around here– I've seen enough television to know that they like the suspect to get so tired they start blurting shit out and confessing.

I can't say that I won't do that, but I haven't yet. So, there's that.

"Ma'am, please, I just have to get this initialed, it's a formality, you're not confessing to anything by doing so." This is from Mr. Good Cop, he's been pretending to be on my side the whole night, telling his partner to ease up on me and offering to get me a glass of water. Again, I've seen this before. T.V. shows these days really give a lot away about how cops operate, they must get some old retired dudes to tell all their secrets and the rest of them are too dumb to switch up their routines.

I know it doesn't mean I'm confessing to anything– and I won't be. I just don't want to do anything they ask of me, I don't want to interact one minute with these dicks. They've gotten to choose the setting for this little powwow they want to have with me and I will obtain the upper hand somehow in this matter. Even if it pisses them off. Let's see how long Mr. Good Cop can keep up his role.

Chapter Two

In the beginning…

Let me start by saying we had an unconventional start to our relationship, I met Matthew in high school, I was a senior that year, and he was my English teacher.

I had shit going on at home and was contemplating dropping out, getting a job and getting the fuck out of there. That was, until I laid my eyes on his beautiful blue ones. My god, I can see them in my memories just as vivid as they were back then. I think I fell in love with him that very instant.

It took him a few weeks for him to notice me, but I knew the moment he did, I saw him see me and then there was this jolt in my soul that would forever change me.

He swept me off my feet and never set me down.

One day after class, he told me that he needed to see me, and my heart swooned. I had imagined those words coming from his mouth every time our eyes met, which was frequently, both of us getting lost in the others for what felt like hours, but really only a few moments would pass before he'd look away. Which would send me into a path of self-doubt, thinking I'd imagined the intensity of our connection, but it would happen again and wash all of that away. He had a way of reassuring me in a second flat.

I sat in my seat and awaited further instructions from him, petrified that what he would say to me would not be that of my fantasies; rather, it would shatter the illusion I had of us. I had to know though, for good or bad, I was ready.

"Please come here, Collette." He sat back into his chair and waited for my stumbling legs to move me forward.

I sat in the seat directly across from him, the desk at his side, our knees practically touching. My hands shook, waiting for my life to change.

"Can I speak frankly with you?"

Oh, *fuck*, this was not going to go in the direction of what I wanted, he was about to tell me that I'd crossed the line and made him uncomfortable, that I was imagining the shit between us.

Still, I nodded, readying myself for the biggest rejection of my life, unable to look at him as he took a deep breath to speak.

"You are a very beautiful girl."

I closed my eyes tightly, afraid that I'd say something so stupid that I would fuck it up somehow by actually acknowledging him. I swallowed my words so hard it hurt my throat, my heart beat so fast I thought it would pump right out of my chest.

"I…" he put his hand on my thigh, just below the hem of my short skirt, well above my knee. "I haven't been able to stop thinking about you." His thumb rubbed my goose- bumped flesh, slipping under the fabric.

I dared, then, to look at him; the ferociousness in his eyes sent a heat through me to my bones. I'd never been more on fire in my life. I parted my legs as my way to confirm that we were on the same page, my voice still unable to speak.

He looked hungry as he pushed his hand between my thighs. "Do you want me to touch you like this?"

All I could do was nod.

"Has anyone ever touched you here like this?"

I cleared my throat, hoping my words would come out stronger than the puddle of lust I felt. "I'm not a virgin, but nobody has touched me like this before."

His fingers rubbed against my panties, sending shivers down my body. I couldn't hold back the whimper that creeped forward as he moved them rhythmically.

"Collette," he waited until I looked at him before continuing. "Do you want me to be inside of you?"

"Uh huh."

"Stand up."

Oh, fuck, I couldn't remember how to use my legs, my knees were so weak, but I had managed, after pulling my attention away from him for a moment, to focus on the task.

"I look at you sometimes and I think of how good it would feel to be inside of you– buried so deep that I'd get lost in you." He pulled my body against his and wrapped his fingers in my hair, pulling my face upward to his, his kiss so hard it almost hurt, but I welcomed the pain– it took some of the focus away from the throbbing ache inside me.

I dragged my hands across his body, touching him everywhere. The fantasies I'd had of him were nothing compared to the way he felt in real life.

He was only a few years older than I was, this was his first year teaching, but his hands knew what to do with my body. He took his time kissing me before progressing, and when he finally did, it excited me through to every nerve ending. I felt exhilarated when he slid his hand between us and into my panties. I'd come in only minutes.

He took my hand and placed it against the hardness in his pants, it felt so good to touch him there.

I was so naïve then, but in that moment, I felt just how it was supposed to be between two people. Unable to contain any ounce of dignity, and not caring to try, I got onto my knees, pulled his hardened cock out of his pants, and took it into my mouth.

I watched his face for his reaction to my efforts; I would never be able to forget just how excited he looked, moving my head in harmony with his bucking hips to get himself off. "I want you to taste me so bad, I want to fill your mouth up," he pulled my head away and left my mouth empty and hungry still. "But I need to be inside of you."

I thought I couldn't get more thrilled by anything at that point, but those words drove me crazy.

He lifted my feet up off the floor and directed me to sit on the edge of his desk, the very desk that had been a fixture in my dreams of him.

He spread my legs apart and sunk into me, I was so wet he was able to fill me in one attempt.

"Fuck, Collette, you feel even better than I thought you would, you're so fucking tight… and wet. I never want to leave here."

He moved slowly at first, and just when I'd thought I would die from his patience, he started to pound me, pushing harder and harder until I felt myself fall over the edge, crying out with my orgasm.

He wasn't done though, he slowed again, kissing me sweetly across my neck and down to my tits, after he'd lifted my shirt to expose them. I wasn't wearing a bra– I never did, he moaned his approval. "I didn't think you were wearing one, I've been lost in the sight of these hard little nipples since you walked in today." He took turns with them, biting each one hard and then sucking them into his mouth, taking the sting out of it.

He gathered me into his arms and shoved my back against the wall behind us. He continued fucking me until I almost couldn't bear another second, and that's when he came, he filled my pussy with his warm come and it felt like heaven to know a part of him would be inside of me even after his cock was gone.

He put me on my feet and situated my panties to cover me again. "Are you on the pill, Collette?"

I nodded.

"Good girl, I won't be able to come anywhere else after feeling you around me."

"Mr. Winthrop?"

He leaned into my ear, "after having my cock inside that sweet little mouth of yours, you'll need to call me Matthew, unless of course you'd like to keep this more professional?" He sucked my ear into his mouth, nibbling the lobe.

I gave some thought to what it would be like after that day, and professional was the furthest thing from my mind. "Matthew?"

"Yes, Collette?" His kisses didn't stop.

"I need to get home, I'm so sorry, but my mother is strict and she'll be wondering where I am if I'm not home soon." I looked up at the big clock on the wall and realized she'd probably already be expecting me.

"Ok, Collette, you may go, but I'll need to see you tomorrow, tell your mother you have a project to work on, have her call me if she needs verification."

"Ok."

I did just that, and we were able to keep our relationship a secret for the rest of the year– through to graduation, fucking every chance we got, risking his career every time we did.

And he was never concerned about it, he told me he wanted me more than his job, he wanted me more than *anything*. I, myself, couldn't stop if I tried, my body was addicted to his, craving him only moments after having him.

I left my mother's house the day of graduation, moving into his condo across town and I never looked back. We were married in December that same year.

I couldn't think without him near, wasn't able to function unless he was inside of me, and the same could be said for him, he was just as hungry for me.

We spent those first few years in a sort of limbo, dividing time between the 'real world' and the next time we could fuck. We spent every moment together fucking until sleep took us for the night, waking to do it all over again. We were like nymphos, craving more and more of each other. It never grew old, I never lost that need for him and I could see how ravenous he always was for me.

But, after the accident things were not the same. They weren't happy times anymore.

Chapter Three

Today...

    "Mrs. Winthrop, despite the fact that you refuse to acknowledge that you've been read your rights we still must proceed with questioning. We have it on video when Detective Patterson read them to you." This is coming from 'bad cop'– even his tone is condescending.

I still say nothing; I don't want these assholes to even know I can speak, let alone hearing what I would have to say on this matter.

"Ma'am, we found your husband dead. Your silence is confusing us, if you had nothing to do with his death, why won't you speak up so we can clear you of any wrong doing?"

Sadly, me speaking would not rule me out. I didn't kill my husband, not directly, anyway.

"We found him in his wheelchair, in your house, with you at home. Surely, you knew he was dead, it looks like it has been weeks since his passing. The worst you could be charged with is 'accessory after the fact', being that you knew he was dead and didn't report it, that's only if you knew nothing of how he came to die.

"I could overlook that and not charge you if you can prove you weren't at fault, but the only way to do that, is for you to speak with us. That's a deal I wouldn't pass up, your husband is badly decomposing and the smell is noxious, we have no doubt you knew he was in there festering. So bad, in fact, that it's hard for the M.E. to confirm cause of death just yet, but trust me, Mrs. Winthrop, he will find that out. And it would behoove you to help us in the meantime or reap the consequences your silence brings."

Wow, that was quite a spiel; I'll take my chances with my silence. They do say it's golden.

I stare at him for more time than my eyes want to focus, but I want to show him how steadfast I am in keeping my silence. Not even to ask for an attorney. I have nothing to say.

The knock on the door concludes our staring contest, and I'm glad for the interruption, until I hear the words that I know mean they've found what I'd been waiting for them to see.

Some guy, I've not had the 'pleasure' of meeting, peeks his head in and glances my way before quickly averting his eyes to look at the detective. "Sir, there's something you need to see." He avoids my eyes on the way out.

Chapter Four

The accident...

Matthew was coming home from work one night, the fifteen- minute drive he would usually spend watching me via his phone on a webcam he had set up at home when he couldn't be near. I would get started before he walked in, putting on a show for him so he could make the drive better and build the anticipation.

I would do a little strip tease for him or fuck myself with his choice of toys, this particular day he wanted to watch me finger myself; it was his favorite. Occasionally, he would join in and jack off, knowing he would be ready for me again when he walked through the door.

I remember being so lost in my show for him I hadn't realized he was no longer responding. A lost connection was nothing new. The minutes ticked by until I realized too much time passed. I stopped immediately and called him.

Voicemail.

Fuck.

I became instantly worried, panic hit me in the gut like a fist. I knew something had happened to him. I felt it in my core. I paced the floor until I got a call, the call I knew was coming, not from Matthew, from the hospital.

"Mrs. Winthrop, this is Kate, I'm a nurse at First Presbyterian Hospital, your husband has been brought in, he's in surgery right now to repair some of the damage resulting from a car accident he was in earlier tonight."

"Thank you, I'll be there as soon as I can."

"I doubt he'll be ready for visitors, but if he asks, I'll tell him you're on your way here. Do you need the address?"

"No, I have it. Thank you."

I had no emotion; I had known something had happened– at least I knew then that he was alive. I could deal with anything else but death, which I could not have gotten over. That… whatever shape he was in, I could deal with that. I would make sure he was ok; I would help him heal from that.

Getting to the hospital that night took more out of me than anything I had ever faced. Dread weighted me down as I trudged along to the waiting room the nurse directed me.

He was still in surgery, although they said he would make it, most of the damage was to his legs and back. They had to rush him in with a specialist to remove some of the swelling that was happening on his spine. They were worried about nerve damage, which they said, could lead to paralysis.

After he got out of surgery, almost eight hours later, the doctor came out to talk to me; I knew it was bad by the look on his face. The words that followed were as bad as they had feared. He would be a paraplegic; they had determined that most if not all feeling was gone from his chest down, narrowly escaping becoming quadriplegic. The doctor told me if the nerves damaged were slightly higher, he wouldn't have had control over his arms.

I sobbed there, in that waiting room, for hours before being told I could go back in and see him. I dreaded the sight of him, or more so, him seeing me for the first time, my pity would be evident across my face. I've never been one to be able to hide my emotions, my reaction would set a precedent for how this would go, how he would see himself through my eyes from that day forward.

I didn't want him to feel anything but loved, so I set my face in the most loving way I could and I opened his door, and my god, it was the worst thing I could see. I almost ran out of the room– for his sake not mine. I couldn't let him know how sorry I felt for him, how badly I wished it hadn't happened. That was our life now and I wanted him to think I was strong enough to handle it.

Luckily, he was not looking at the door as I came through, I was able to fix my expression and call to him before he looked at me.

"Matthew…"

"Hey, love." He sounded like himself, even if he didn't quite look like himself, not that there was damage to be seen, but just the machines he had to be hooked up to and the way that I could tell it wasn't the same man lying in that bed, my heart was breaking.

"Has the doctor been through your prognosis with you?" I didn't really want to be the one to tell him, but I couldn't sit here another second not knowing whether he knew.

"Yea, seems I really fucked myself up." Those are the same words he would have used before this calamity, but the inflection of those words was different, they didn't hold the same humor.

"Do you need me to get you anything?" They said he'd need a while to recuperate, a lot of internal damage took place in that car.

"Could you just sit with me? I've missed you more than I thought possible." Those words melted me to the core, maybe not all was lost and maybe I could find him in there again.

I did sit with him that night, for hours, in silence, neither of us knowing quite what to say.

Chapter Five

Home…

We had gotten home from the hospital, where every moment I could feel things becoming awkward and strained, however that did not measure up to how it was once I had gotten him back.

I had put all my hope into that moment that that time would be behind us and right away, I could feel that things had not changed.

Almost a month spent getting him ready for that day so he could return, but he was no longer the man I had married, a new version of the man I had fallen head over heels in love with had snuck into him, wearing his skin, changing him into a fucked up version of my beloved.

"Matthew, I got everything set up for you, everything is wheelchair accessible now, but if you need help I'm right here for you."

"Thanks," he grumbled.

I could tell he was angry, although I couldn't pinpoint if it was at me or the predicament he was in. I blamed myself for his accident; I didn't know how he could *not*. There was a lot of guilt building inside of me for what happened that night, thoughts running wild inside my head, circling around, all of the things that could have happened differently; they played on a continuous loop through my conscience.

Had we not become so engaged in the sex-play he may not have lost focus and driven head first into that telephone pole, which, as luck would have it, hadn't stopped the car's momentum, he flipped the jeep countless times after.

With no witnesses on the scene, it was hard to know for sure what happened. It had knocked him unconscious and it was a while before someone stopped to phone police, his nerves where dying while he lay there waiting. I was the source of the distraction and my guilt wouldn't let me forget that.

I regretted my decision to not go out and check on him after I had realized he was late and possibly in trouble. I had never really been clear headed in times of stress or worry, that was always Matthew's job.

I went about making him as comfortable as possible, bending over backwards to accommodate him. Going forward, I chose not to ask him if he did blame me for what had become of him.

I could only serve him for my penance– every meal, every bath, every time he had a fucking phantom itch, I was there to ease the burden.

We had settled into that routine quickly– me his servant, and him the poor man who had lost the ability to function from the chest down. Luckily, he hadn't lost the use of his arms, although sometimes the nerves inside them made it very painful to use them.

I was just grateful for his life– he, perhaps, was not. I knew he would have preferred death over what he got that night. He said sometimes, that he wished his broken and useless body would wither and die, but the doctors all had hope for him to have a normal life– whatever the fuck that was.

Days went by, I tried so hard to love this new man, the grouchy, and often times, mean and cold shell that my sweet Matthew used to wear, this stranger had taken over and begun using it.

The night I knew it was over for sure was about three years after the accident; I was trying, as I often did, to satisfy the man he was in bed. He still had a voracious appetite for sex. He had the sex drive of the man I remembered late at night in my fantasies, the man he was before. He said he couldn't feel it like he used to but his cock worked and in his words, "it's the only thing that could get up from this fucking chair". I, being the dutiful wife to a paralyzed man who had become so low and depressed, wanted nothing more than to satisfy him.

This night I lay him back onto the bed, rubbing his legs to stimulate the blood flow, sometimes it helped, and I always tried my hardest to do everything I could to help ease him through that time of our lives. I still loved him, despite the miserable man making himself at home inside my husband.

We had always been at our best when we were fucking, I knew we were meant to be from the first time he had taken me inside his classroom, the chemistry had always been there. It had fizzled a little after the chair, but not so much so that it wasn't still the hottest sex. Or so *I* thought.

I put on a cute little tee and some barely- there undies, slid up his body to kiss him, then made my way down his chest to his hardening cock, he was still so responsive. I took it onto my mouth and sucked it hard, making sure to keep my eyes on him the way I knew he liked.

I pulled my panties over to the side and sunk down onto his slick cock, grinding on the top of his lap. He groped me, grabbing my tits– his favorite part of me.

"You feel so good, baby." I told him, completely lost in the feeling. "Rub my pussy for me." It's something he loved to hear me say, it always turned him on to have me hungry for his touch.

I saw something flash in his eyes, something I hadn't noticed before, I saw hatred, it had me regretting my words immediately, although I couldn't understand why. "You need to make sure you're getting me off, too." His words were so full of anger.

My chin quivered, holding back tears that were right on the edge of falling out. I hadn't realized how selfish I might have sounded.

"Of course, Matthew." I made my best attempt at a smile, but I knew it wasn't a success.

"Get off of me, you whore. You don't even care about me, you only want more and more. I can't even feel *anything* and you want to feel *everything*– you greedy slut."

I ran from our room, leaving him naked on our bed. I couldn't bring myself to come back in for hours. I sat in the bathtub, the hot water turning cold, crying all the tears I had been holding in so I could show a brave face to my husband.

I began to feel bad for leaving, those words were harsh, more mean than I've heard him ever speak, but I realized he was frustrated and what kind of wife would I be if I couldn't support him in his condition. Our vows very clearly stated that it was for better or worse, sickness and health. And although this wasn't quite sickness– it was *worse*, and I had made him a promise. So, I stood and dressed, then made my way back into our room to tend to him.

I feel utterly embarrassed to say the next part, but I need to explain the progression his anger was taking.

I walked in the door, tail between my legs, ready to apologize, but what I was met with was him fuming. "Get the fuck over here, Collette." He pushed his words through gritted teeth.

I walked to him hesitantly. Against my better judgement, I sat next to him on the bed. He reached up and grabbed me hard by the hair. "You think it's ok to leave me in here to fucking piss on myself?"

Shame flushed through me, radiating more pain inside me than his hand fisted inside my hair. "I'm so sorry." I truly felt so bad for causing that to happen.

"You want to make me feel like a piece of shit? You want to degrade me and show me that I'm scum? Well, it fucking worked. I pissed all over."

He pulled my head down and I could do nothing but follow him, he tugged hard until my face was level with the wet mattress and he shoved my face into it. He didn't let me up for long enough that I began to panic, I couldn't breathe, which made me gasp, forcing the urine in through my nose and mouth and into my lungs.

His arms were the only part of him that hadn't been deteriorating, they'd actually gotten stronger from using his chair. I couldn't escape, not without ripping the hair from my head. So, I just lay there, struggling to breathe, feeling that was going to be my end. I was going to die there with my face shoved in a puddle of my husband's piss.

I couldn't help but think it was my fault, so when I forgave him for it, I thought that I could avoid things like that happening again if only I was good enough. But no matter what I did, it wasn't good enough, not right enough. I still suffered his wrath. Where before the accident he could see no wrong in me, afterward he could see no right.

It broke my heart, shattered it to pieces on an almost daily basis– until I had no heart at all. It was an unrecognizable thing that stopped feeling and had become something that just pumped blood. I couldn't find an ounce of compassion for him. I couldn't find a flicker of love.

On our tenth anniversary I had realized I'd spent more time with him in this condition, (I'm not speaking of the wheelchair– I could have loved him forever in whatever shape I was blessed to have him in) I mean the cold, heartless, and hating man he had become after. The weight shifted inside of me when I realized I'd been with him happy less time than I'd been with him miserable and mistreated.

I felt something take hold inside of me, some vengeful thoughts that hated him for taking the man that I loved and morphing him into this man– if I could call him a man, a real man wouldn't do the things he had done to the woman he supposedly loved.

Chapter Six

After that dawned on me I couldn't help him anymore, I couldn't keep waiting around for him to become something else– the man he was before. I felt I had given him enough time to change and become accommodated to his new life. He'd taken enough from me and I was done giving.

I went about my duties as if I was a nurse; I made sure he had everything he needed: food, shelter, bathroom, showers. Everything else fell away and he didn't ask why. He did not attempt to inquire and I gave no answers to him.

On this particular day, he had taken it upon himself to get out of bed alone; he had done it on occasion with my supervision– he really had become quite strong and self- reliant. It would have been impressive if I still cared.

I heard the crash from the kitchen, the walls shook as if a bomb had gone off, and I ran so fast into the room. He was lying on the floor in a crumpled heap.

It's hard enough for me to maneuver him when he is in his chair or on the bed, it is nearly impossible for me to deadlift him off the floor. I tried and tried until the sweat was mixing with the tears streaming from my eyes; he called me names, made me feel awful, and blamed me for that happening, saying that I had left his chair unlocked.

I felt like I wanted to curl up into a ball and drown my pain in a big bottle of some mind-numbing alcohol. Instead, I took a deep breath and heaved him up until he could grab the arms of his chair and help me the rest of the way.

I practically fell on top of him as I released his weight and plopped him down, having exerted all my strength. I regretted it instantly as he used his favorite move– grabbing me by the hair– it incapacitated me right away.

He didn't speak, his breath was coming as hard as mine, but he hadn't exhausted all his energy, he still had some reserved for my face, which he struck repeatedly until I couldn't feel my head, it was swollen and bleeding freely from more than one gash, swelling my eyes shut almost immediately.

There was so much blood coming from my face that I hadn't noticed he was also hurt. I didn't notice until that night, when I undressed him to shower, that he had cut his back on something left on the floor. It was a fairly deep laceration and by the time I found it, it had not closed.

I put him on the bathroom chair and sat on the toilet seat to tend to it.

He seemed really annoyed at me for neglecting to find it earlier, like I wasn't busy enough with my own shit.

With my eyes still swollen shut, I attempted to clean his wound. The anger in me was growing, he didn't feel his pain and I was struggling to overcome mine. I was growing resentful, even more so after having to care for him while he was the cause of mine. It didn't seem fair.

I wiped the blood without a care; he, of course, didn't feel it either way, so to get back at him, I didn't do it nicely.

I wanted to gouge him, dig my finger inside of his cut, to make him feel it and, before I could stop myself, did. I pushed my finger along the incision and I felt vindication, I felt stronger inflicting him with that. I didn't care that he couldn't feel it.

"Hurry the fuck up, how fucking long is this going to take you?" I hated him so much, I couldn't even respond.

I didn't care that he was impatient, I just pushed deeper into his flesh until blood poured out, dripping down his back. I crooked my finger and slide it between his skin and the meaty flesh underneath; it went easily, like I was skinning a chicken breast. I did that around the perimeter of the cut. My hands were shaking, and the excitement of the mutilation gave me quite an exhilarating rush.

I slowed my breathing and calmed myself so I could carry on, cleaning and bandaging the cut quickly after I was done. He was none the wiser and I had felt great. It almost made up for what he had done to my face.

Almost.

I slept great that night, lying next to him with my little secret keeping me company.

Chapter Seven

Today...

"We found some questionable marks on your husband's body. Before we get started with those things, do you care to explain what you think they might be?" he walks through the door asking, setting down a manila folder, which I assume to be photos of what he's talking about.

I say nothing; nothing could explain what they have found. I can't explain why I did those things, even to myself. How would I be able to form the words to say it aloud to him?

Chapter Eight

What they'd found in the photos...

It didn't stop there. His abuse or mine toward him. A part of me looked forward to him hurting me so I could retaliate. His evolution of abuse and mistreatment of me fed my own.

He would call me over to him, and expected me to stand there as I took his punches, and I would, I would stand there and let him hit me, let him manhandle me. After a while, he kept them aimed away from my face, learning quickly that I couldn't still leave the house to run the errands he demanded of me.

If he was able bodied, I'm sure rape would have followed, he had gotten hard on more than one occasion. It repulsed me– fed my hate.

I had waited for that beating to be over, then I went over to the kitchen sink, grabbing the first knife I saw, and jabbed it into his back. He hadn't even moved, so I'd done it again. Three times in total, three slits half an inch wide and about an inch deep, dripping blood down his shirt. I didn't even bother bandaging them or the ones that would follow– I couldn't necessarily let on about what was going on literally behind his back.

At night, while he slept, I would push my fingers into them or trace along the scars of the older ones.

Once, I had become so angry with him for sleeping so peacefully, that I pushed a thumbtack into him; a blue one that was on my nightstand, in and out to my heart's content– the popping of his flesh each time I did it seemed to calm me. There must have been hundreds of little tiny little blood dots.

He woke me up that morning, not in the usual way, not demanding I take him to the bathroom so he doesn't have an accident, no, that morning I woke up being suffocated with his hand. It surprised me more than anything else that he got the leverage to prop himself up into a position to do it. He rarely let on about his strength, unless he was using it to abuse me. He had always demanded I do everything for him, claiming he wasn't able to himself.

I pulled free of him easily by simply sliding off the bed away from him. "You are so fucking stupid. Who the fuck were you going to call for help after you killed me? Not thinking too smart, you dipshit."

I left the room, not letting him respond. I put on my coat and left the house to escape him.

Whatever happened after that was completely on him– or on the mattress, so to speak.

I regretted it the second I walked back into the room that evening. He was lying on the floor again, having fallen from the bed again, in a puddle of piss. He was furious.

I was scared to go close to him; I knew that it would be a bad beating for sure. So, I avoided it as long as possible. I turned and left him; walking into the kitchen to make dinner. I thought that maybe he would be thinking of food and want to eat; maybe it would postpone the inevitable.

I brought the plate of food into him, setting it on the nightstand. "If I pick you up off the floor are you going to hurt me?"

"No. Just get me the fuck up."

"If you so much as *think* about hurting me, I will throw your food away and leave you on the floor."

"Just pick me the fuck *up*, you bitch."

"You're lucky that didn't hurt my feelings."

"Whatever," he mumbled.

I got Matthew into his chair without incident and rolled him over to the stand so he could collect his plate. I turned to go make one for myself when the plate hit the back of my head. I fell to the floor before I knew a reason for the pain. I passed out; I remember waking up without knowing right away my reason for being on the floor.

"What the fuck?" I shook my head and felt more pain than I ever had before. I had landed face down on the hardwood. The blood seeping out of my head dripped down my face, flooding my eyes and drying before I woke.

"It tasted like shit." He shrugged his shoulders, completely un-phased by what he'd done.

I felt the back of my head and my finger landed along the gouge. It was deep; too deep to close itself, I knew I needed stitches. I got myself ready, without a word to Matthew and drove to the emergency room where I sat fuming, boiling over with rage. I needed to hurt him.

If it was bad before, after that it was worse, I couldn't even stand the sight of him. I returned home with sixteen staples in the back of my head. I had to make up a lie to tell the nurse when she looked horrified while questioning me about what had happened. I felt embarrassed. I know I could have gone to the police, maybe I should have, but I'd done some things to him as well, things I couldn't explain away.

I returned home and he instantly began shouting for me. I couldn't bring myself to go into the room just then, so I sat on the couch and listened to him until he stopped.

He could have simply come out of the room, if he really wanted to, the whole house was accessible to him, but he chose not to. So I left him.

The night came and went, still nothing from him. I didn't sleep, my head hurt too much. My mind was spinning with thoughts of the old days, the before times that were so good that they made me really know what love was. Hate took my feet toward him; he was asleep in the bed.

I glared at his sleeping body, boiling with hatred. I walked up to him, grabbed him, and pulled him off the bed; he hit the floor with a thud. I took him by the arms and dragged him to the basement door, then opened it, and against my desire to roll him down the stairs, I instead, eased him down one by one, his feet crashing down on each step.

"What the fuck are you doing?" he asked when struggling and fighting against me weren't working.

I didn't answer, my voice wouldn't work. Plus, I didn't really have an explanation as much as a compulsion to do that. I turned and left him lying on the cold and dirty floor, alone in the dark room for hours before returning to check on him.

He was shouting when I opened the door, demanding I put him back in is his chair and feed him. He didn't say anything about taking him upstairs, probably knowing his attempts would be futile.

I went back up to retrieve his chair and brought it down the darkened stairs to him. I thought about just killing him. Not like the times I had done so before, this time, I had a clear image of me walking over to him and gutting him.

The thing that stopped me was unclear. I don't know why I didn't go through with it then. Instead, I loaded him onto his chair, he had no idea how close he'd come to drawing his last breath just then, if he had, maybe he wouldn't have done what he did next.

As I was walking away from him, he grabbed onto my thigh and I fell face first onto the floor. That was the last straw, as I picked myself up for the last fucking time I vowed to end him. I didn't have anything left holding me back, that thread that tethered me to him snapped the second my chin bounced off the concrete floor.

"I'll be back down in a minute with your food." My voice sounded strange, even to me, it wasn't the same as it had been all those miserable years, it was the old me, she came through just then, and it felt like she was saving me, rescuing me from this shithole my life had become.

I welcomed her as she joined me in making his food, uplifting me in a way I hadn't been able to myself in all that time.

He treated me like a fucking dog, worse than a dog, the shit that comes out of a dog, and that was how I wanted to repay him.

I made chicken marsala that night, served over noodles, it was delicious, what I brought to him were the scraps of my own food: chicken bones mostly, like I said it was delicious, I nearly ate it all.

"What the fuck is this?" he said, when I handed him the plate.

"Shut up and eat it, there won't be anything else tonight." I responded politely as my alter took over again.

Matthew didn't get hungry like you would imagine hunger. He had explained it to me one time–

his brain sort of told him it had been enough hours and he craved food, there would be phantom pains he would feel but not like the old hunger pains, so when he threw the plate across the room shattering it on the wall, I left. He probably wouldn't miss it anyway.

I went down in the morning to find him on the floor; he had fallen over reaching for those bones and eaten them where he fell.

"I see you decided to eat."

He didn't respond.

"Do you want back in your chair or not?"

"Yes."

"Yes, what? You lost your manners?"

"Yes, please."

I reached over and patted his head. "Good dog." My tone was belittling, he said nothing, just sort of growled at me. I let it go.

I pulled him up into his chair, noticing some serious cuts on his back and arms from the shattered plate– you would think I'd have learned my lesson about those fucking things, but that was the last plate I gave him so there wouldn't be a third time he could chuck one at me.

"I'll be back down in a minute, don't go anywhere." I sing- songed.

Chapter Nine

Today...

      "Where you Matthew's primary care giver?" They brought back in Mr. Good Cop; I can tell his opinion of me has changed, where he used to look at me with mild confusion and maybe a small amount of pity, now I see a mask covering his disgust. I can't blame him, I was waiting for it to happen.

"Well, as you may know, the M.E. has been giving your husband's body an examination, since you've been no help what so ever by way of answers to what happened to him.

"He found some marks, looks like some older than others, pretty deep lacerations covering his back, you're not going to try and convince me he was just clumsy are you?"

I don't say anything.

"Upon further investigation he found some larger chunks missing, it was really gross; I looked... wish I hadn't. Some of those pieces are a match for what he found in his stomach."

Chapter Ten

Devoured...

I left Matthew down there for weeks; checking on him became far less frequent as the days passed. I couldn't make myself care anymore, everything he said to me added fuel to the fire. He got weaker; I could see him withering away. I didn't feel an ounce of regret for that. I knew the moment I took him down there that I'd never bring him back up, I knew inside that I was sending him away for good.

I snuck down there one night, he was sleeping, as he had been most the time, he became very lethargic, not having energy left.

He was hunched over in the chair, his head nearly touching his knees, wearing the same pair of boxers he'd been wearing when I dragged him there weeks ago.

I went upstairs in a trance, coming back down with the paring knife in my hand, I sort of watched myself cut a moon- shaped half circle into his back, slipping my finger inside it, I pulled the flesh from the meat and cut a palm sized chunk from him.

There were festering wounds covering him, they looked awful: infected, rotting and stinking.

He didn't even move. I would have thought he was already dead if I hadn't heard his shallow breath.

I did the same thing on the other side, pulling the skin back down to cover the crater, then headed back upstairs.

I took out my cast- iron pan, and I fried those pieces of meat, plating them next to green beans and mashed potatoes, and then brought it downstairs for him.

"Eat," I said. I watched as he ate hungrily; choking to get it all down. It must have been longer than I thought since last I fed him something other than my scraps.

"Finally a decent fucking meal." I watched him eat until he popped the last piece of himself into his mouth.

I think a part of me knew that that was the last time I would see him, I don't really know when he died, I didn't go back down there after that to confirm. He got his last meal and I felt that was all that was required of me.

I set about living my life again, doing all the mundane shit that was required of me.

The next thing I knew, about three weeks later, the cops were at my door pushing me aside and claiming they had a search warrant. I wasn't nervous, or scared like you might think I'd be with a man downstairs that I only assumed was dead.

One of the officers that stayed behind told me that some kids found something suspicious in my basement.

I wanted to ask questions, the first being why the fuck were kids poking their noses in my basement, but I didn't. I let him speak.

"They threw a ball and it broke your window, instead of bothering you at your door they snuck in to get it. Creeped them the fuck out to find what they claim was a dead body. We are just here to check it out, can't be too sure. Seemed legitimate though–most kids don't confess to a crime like breaking and entering unless they're really freaked out, you know?"

There were shouts coming from the basement, and I knew what was coming, he took my wrists and cuffed them behind my back.

"Looks like those kids were right." He started in on my rights, leading me to the back of a cruiser.

Chapter Eleven

Today…

     "That is the sickest most disgusting thing I have ever seen, you are one sick lady. You really aren't going to want to take your chances with a jury, they'd feed you to the wolves," Officer Bad Cop says.

     "The M.E. says he must have died from infection, says that that was some of the worst conditions he could have been in. You would have to be pretty heartless to leave a man in like that."

I am heartless. Wheelchair bound Matthew stole my heart, ruined my life and tore me apart repeatedly. I don't feel bad, in fact, I don't feel anything.

Epilogue

My punishment...

Prison is fine I have no complaints. The women in here know what I did to Matthew– news travels fast around here, and they mostly avoid me.

When I hear anyone talking about me, they use the word heinous a lot. I guess I am a kind of monster. I wasn't always, and I miss that girl sometimes. I don't know how to get her back though, I think we both died in the car the night of his accident, neither of us were really the same after that.

Please leave a review, it would be appreciated greatly and only takes a second to let me know what you thought.

Thank you

Printed in Great Britain
by Amazon